WINTER EVE

SHIFTERS OF ASHWOOD FALLS, BOOK ONE

LIA DAVIS

Winter Eve

Shifters of Ashwood Falls, book 1

www.AuthorLiaDavis.com

To the love of my life, for putting up with my craziness.

Winter Eve

There comes a time when setting your differences aside isn't just necessary, it's a means of survival. After losing over half of their dens to a group rogue shifters, the wolves and leopards merged as one Pack, but living together is much more of a challenge then they expected.

Danica Welsh was born to be the leopard pack healer. An accident involving a drug induced youth left her badly burned and scared—emotionally and physically. Without the ability to heal by touch, she secludes herself to the edge of town, away from Ashwood Falls' overly concerned citizens. All hope of mating and family become a distance dream. When she finally starts to accepts the long, lonely existence ahead of her, a stranger crashes into her life, and her heart.

After Nevan Mathews' fiancé died three ago, he submerged himself into his work, cutting off all reminders of a life he dreamed of with the woman he loved. He lets his step-mother talk him into taking the first vacation in five years to visit for the holidays. But an accident delays his travel plans, sending him to Danica's doorstep and raises a need he thought he would never feel again.

Can they tear down the walls around their hearts and submit to the passion before another claims Dani for his own?

1

The winding, slick roads of the Smoky Mountains seemed creepier than the last time Nevan Matthews had traveled them. Then again, at the time, he'd been seven, it was daylight, and there wasn't snow on the ground.

Why was he even going? Oh, right. His extended family would bug the shit out of him if he didn't show up, just like they had bugged him about every aspect of his life since his father's death five years ago. And, again, when his fiancée, Becca, died a year later. The only family he had left in the world had demanded he spend the holiday season with them.

"You need your family now more than ever," Sarah, his stepmother, had said. "You spend too much time alone."

Her soft, pleading voice had tugged at his heart, and he'd finally given in. He loved his stepmother. She'd always cared for him as if he was her own son. It was impossible to say 'no' to the only mother he had ever known. Besides, he hadn't been back home since his father's death. So he took his first vacation in five years to spend the holidays in a place he didn't belong. With people far different from him.

A blur of brown fur zipped in front of his headlights, and he jerked the rental car to the left. His heart hammered in his chest as the car swerved on the icy road and slammed into the rock wall of the mountainside.

Steam rolled from under the smashed hood and mingled with the frigid winter night as Nevan emerged from the car. He cursed under his breath and raked a hand through his light brown hair.

"Now what?"

He scanned the area for signs of life. He figured Sarah's cabin was a good twenty miles away. He'd freeze to death on top of this mountain on a night like this before reaching the cabin on foot.

Movement to his right caught his attention, and he narrowed his eyes for a better look. A large leopard crouched, staring at him from the roadside. With eyes that reflected the full moon's light, the creature blinked and let out a soft growl before it turned to walk up a gravel driveway.

The animal was beautiful, scary, and its eyes held a hint of humanity. Could it be a were? Sarah hadn't said anything about others living this far up the mountain. When the beast turned to look at him, he swore it wanted him to follow. He took a step forward, and the cat started walking again.

"Oh, great, Nev. You're being lead away by a cat, like Alice and that damn rabbit," he muttered to himself. No one would ever believe him. In fact, it was probably leading him to the den to share with the rest of the pack. Shaking his head at the ridiculous thought, he walked up the driveway. The cat sped up, running ahead much too fast for him. Then it darted into the woods a few feet from a single-story log cabin nestled into the surrounding trees. Another step caused a blinding light to click on, illuminating the front of the yard and the cabin. A few moments later, the door opened, revealing the most beautiful woman he'd ever seen. She stepped out onto the large wide porch. Her straight silk-like strawberry blond hair cascaded over her shoulders and stopped at her waist. The light of the full moon cast against her pale skin made her look like a goddess.

"What can I do to help you?"

Her velvety smooth voice warmed his body and awoke a very specific part of his anatomy. It was several seconds before he found his voice and shook out of the trance she'd cast upon him. "I crashed my car and wondered if you have a phone. My cell doesn't get service up here."

"I don't have a phone." Her gaze left him to search their surroundings and stopped as she glanced toward the dark sky as though she saw something he didn't, or couldn't, see. "But, come inside. You'll freeze to death in the storm." She turned and walked back inside.

Storm?

A single snowflake drifted in front of his face, landing on his nose.

DANICA CROSSED the living room to the fireplace, feeling the man's stare like tiny caresses over her skin. After grabbing the poker, she stirred the fire and added another log. Keegan would freaking flip if he knew she'd taken in a stranger, especially a human stranger, but there was something about this human. "What's your name?"

There was a pause, and then he let out a husky reply, as if startled by the question. "Nevan"

"I'm Danica." She stood and held out her left hand to him. Not because this stranger had uncovered long-buried desires, and she'd been much too long without a male's touch. Nope, that wasn't it at all. She simply wanted to see if he could be trusted. Sniffing out a lie or even the barest hint of dishonesty was like a shifter's sixth sense. Other shifters didn't have troubles detecting a lie from across the room, but Danica's sense of smell had been damaged along with most of the right side of her body in a fire a couple of years before. It was one reason she lived on the edge of town, away from the others' pity.

"Nice to meet you." There was a hesitation in his voice and leeriness in his gaze.

"What brings you up the mountain this late in the season?"

"I was on my way to my stepmother's for the holidays." A frown creased his forehead. "Do you know where there's a phone? I should call before she sends out the cavalry."

"Cavalry?"

"My stepbrothers."

"How many do you have?"

"Four. Three of them are older, and one is a year younger than me."

She hid her smile by turning toward the kitchen. "That's a big family." In this day and age, humans didn't usually have large families. The ones that did held more family values than those who didn't. They were more likely to protect each other.

She walked into the kitchen and started a pot of coffee. When she turned around, she was startled by the sight of Nevan standing just a few feet away. She reached out to balance herself only to find Nevan beside her faster than she'd expected a human to move. He took her elbow and she gasped at the heat of his body so close to hers. Her body warmed, and her pulse increased. With only a few inches separating them, she could smell his natural male scent mixed with his aftershave. Spicy and good enough to lick all over…

She took a few steps back. He was a stranger, for God's sake. She wasn't the seducing type. Besides, who would want to make love to a scarred, half-powered leopard?

"I'm sorry, I didn't mean to scare you."

"I didn't hear you move." Which was crazy considering there was nothing wrong with her supernatural hearing. She poured coffee into two cups and handed him one, careful not to make physical contact again. Leaning against the counter, she studied him. He was human. Nothing remotely magickal or paranormal about him, yet there was something in the way he carried himself and moved.

Shaking her head, she shifted to peer out the window. The snow was coming down in sheets. "Looks like we're in for the night."

Fabric sliding over fabric indicated he'd moved closer to look out the window. "At least."

She lifted her gaze to meet his. He smiled, and she thought her knees would give out. Stepping around him before she completely embarrassed herself, she walked out of the kitchen. "Come, I'll show you to the guest room and get some extra blankets."

The trip down the hall was the longest in her two hundred twenty-three years of life. The male following her put her cat on edge.

Stopping at the linen closet, she grabbed sheets and a couple of blankets and handed them to him. She quickly turned into the bedroom to her left. "The shower is across the hall, and there is firewood on the back porch. Would you like me to get you some?"

"No. I think I can manage." He offered her another gentle smile, and the air in the room grew thick.

"I'll leave you to clean up. I'm kind of a night creature, so I hope I won't disturb you."

He looked around the room before meeting her stare again. "Thank you."

"You're welcome," she said softly and walked back down the hallway toward the living room. It was her fault he was here, stranded. If she hadn't darted in front of his car like an irresponsible cub, he'd be on his way to see his family.

An all-too-familiar energy nudged at her psyche, and her mood lifted. She went straight to the front door and opened it before Shayna Andrews could knock. "Why on earth are you here in this weather?"

Laughing, the beautiful blond stomped her snow covered boots on the porch and entered the cabin. "I was hunting and wondered a little too far out, and then it started snowing, suddenly."

Danica shook her head. Shay was always testing her adopted brothers' abilities to track her. She liked to see how far from town she'd get before they caught up to her. "Doesn't pissing your brothers off get old?"

A mischievous smile lifted the side of her mouth. "Nope. But, this time, I was actually hunting. You know how focused I can get in cat form."

"Yeah. That focused curiosity is going to get you in trouble." Danica motioned to the kitchen and frowned. She'd advised Keegan to allow Shay out of town to learn to use her skills for the Packs. But, no, the Alpha leopard refused to let his princess out of his sight. It was a shame that a twenty-five-year-old tiger shifter had to be under guard 24/7. Keegan was blinded by the fear he'd lose her the way he'd lost his mate during the attacks on the den over two centuries ago.

"Speaking of your brothers…"

"Blaine should be here in about three seconds."

Danica shook her head again. It always surprised her how much Shay was in tune to her adopted brothers. Then she froze. "Did you say Blaine?"

"Yeah…hey, you have a male here." Shay walked toward the hall, sniffing the air. "And he's human. Way to go, Dani!"

Cursing, Danica tugged at her arm. "Please don't. It's not what you think. I caused his car to crash. I'm taking him into town tomorrow to use a phone."

Shaking her head, Shay locked gazes with her. "You can't bring a human into Ashwood Falls. Father will have a wolf."

Danica dropped her shoulders. "I have no choice."

"You could've left the human alone." The deep, stern male voice made her wince, but didn't surprise her. She felt the leopard's presence about two seconds ago.

"I'm a healer, Blaine."

Blaine leaned his large frame against the counter, one dark brow raised. "Was he hurt?"

"No."

"Then he was none of your concern."

Danica's patience with the Enforcer was growing very thin. "You're wrong. He's none of *your* concern. This is *my* house."

He growled. "I know that. You are family, Pack. It's my job to ensure everyone is safe. Inviting a human into your home is not safe, for any of us."

She folded her arms over her chest. "And, I still have the ability to detect the good in people."

"Damn it, Dani—"

Shay pushed by her brother, cutting off his sentence and making him turn toward the entrance of the kitchen. Danica followed his gaze to Nevan.

Shay had her hand out-stretched. "Hi. I'm Shay."

"Nevan." He shook her hand, looked from Blaine to Danica. "Is everything okay?"

Danica shoved past the mountain of an Enforcer to stand between the two males. "Blaine was just leaving."

Blaine studied Nevan for several moments

without speaking. Cocking her head to the side, she noticed a faint expression of…acceptance? Surely, she was tired and didn't just witness the alpha male in front of her dismissing an argument.

Finally, he peered down at her and smiled weakly. He lifted her right hand and pressed her scarred palm to his cheek, a sign of trust and respect among the Pack. "Are you sure you don't need anything?"

She rested her free hand over his heart. "No. I appreciate your concern."

That arrogant smile he was famous for made its slow appearance. "Bring your friend over for a late lunch tomorrow to meet father."

She rolled her eyes and ignored the command in the voice. "Good night, Blaine."

Chuckling, he moved to the front door. Shay drew her in a tight hug and whispered, "Sorry," before following her brother outside.

Danica locked the door behind them. She wasn't sure if Shay was apologizing for Blaine being an ass or for the fact that she would have to put Nevan through a meeting with the Pack Alpha. Knowing her, it was both.

"Your brother?"

Confused, she turned to meet his gray-colored gaze. "What?'

"Blaine. Is he your brother?"

"Oh. I guess you could say that. We grew up together. His family took me in when my parents died." She thought about it for a moment. Warmth entered her heart, filling it with unconditional love. The Andrews were her family. "Yeah, I guess he is the brother I never had. Over protective and all."

He laughed and peered out the window, and the seriousness returned to his handsome features. "It's snowing hard. How did they get here?"

She moved to the sink to clean the cups and avoid his curious stare. Damn. She couldn't tell him the truth, and she didn't want to lie to him. Blaine was one of the rare shifters who could teleport. The ability was limited to places he'd been before and to follow someone he had a blood bond with, like family or a mate. "Blaine has a truck that can drive through anything." Which was true, but she doubted he'd driven it tonight.

Suddenly, Nevan was standing beside her, taking a cup to dry it. She jumped. "How do you do that?"

"Do what?"

"Move without a sound."

He shrugged but didn't look at her. "My brothers have very good hearing. I kind of grew up trying to sneak past them."

She laughed at the mischief in his tone.

He fell quiet, making her glance his way. His gaze drifted over the scars on her right arm before meeting her eyes. "What happened?"

Setting the cup in the drainer, she pushed her sleeves down and shook her head. "I...I'm tired. Sorry." She walked around him and fled to her room. Heart pounding in her chest, she leaned against the closed door.

She was a complete idiot. Damn him for raising hope that any male would find her attractive.

2

Nevan woke to the smoky scent of bacon and the rich aroma of fresh coffee. He sat up and swung his legs over the edge of the bed. Scrubbing his hands over his face, he cursed. What was he doing? His behavior last night was not only uncalled for but completely out of character.

He'd flirted with Danica and enjoyed it. She hadn't, however. He should have picked up on her uneasiness before his curiosity had sent her away. The need to know everything about her was strong. Too strong. He'd never been so intrigued by a woman before. Not even Becca.

Becca.

A lump formed in his throat as her smiling face

entered his mind. So full of life. Until the day she fell ill.

Shaking his head, he stood and noticed his suitcase on the floor next the nightstand. He clenched his teeth together at the thought of Danica going out in the snow to bring his bag inside. He walked to the window, moved the curtain, and peered out at the blanket of white snow covering the ground and trees. *At least it stopped snowing.*

Turning from the window, he grabbed fresh pair of jeans and a long sleeve shirt, then made his way to the kitchen where the delicious smells of breakfast beckoned him.

Danica stood at the stove flipping a pancake, dressed in a pair of black jeans that looked like they were painted on her long legs and a white turtleneck sweater that hung to mid-thigh. Her strawberry blond hair was braided down her back, revealing the scars peaking out of her sweater under her ear. He guessed she hid them from everyone.

Many burn victims he'd worked with hid their scars because the emotional ones were enough to deal with. They didn't want the physical reminders. He should have known better than ask about them.

"I was working at the hospital in town, helping

with a drug-addicted youth," she said as she handed him a bottle of syrup and a plate with three pancakes.

"You don't have to explain. It was insensitive of me to ask. I'm sorry."

She smiled. "No, I'm sorry. I'm not used to strangers. Everyone in town knows and avoids talking about it."

"Is that why you live here alone?"

She nodded. "They drove me crazy with concern and pity."

He couldn't help but think there was more to it, something she wasn't saying. But he let it drop. It wasn't his business.

"I don't remember much. One minute we were talking the male down and the next he freaked out, then there was an explosion. I woke up ten days later, scars littering the right side of my body." She turned back to the stove. The hesitation as she spoke told him she was leaving pieces out. Something his brothers and Sarah did when they were around humans.

They carefully planned every word to avoid alluding to the fact they were different.

Nev, you're losing it.

"I lost my dad to a car accident five years ago and

my fiancée a year later." He wasn't sure why he was telling her, but it felt good to talk to someone outside his family, he continued, "I turned to my work and away from my stepmother and brothers."

She faced him now and held his gaze with the palest green eyes he'd ever seen. "I'm so sorry."

He shrugged, trying to push away the pain that threatened to consume him. "I agreed to spend the holidays with my family, hoping it would heal some of the loss."

"How did she die?"

A dull ache formed in his chest threatening to bring back the buried pain. "Becca had leukemia. She died before a bone marrow donor was found."

She reached over and covered his hand with her scarred one. "Oh, no."

He absently stroked her palm with his thumb. "She was ill for a very long time. I took care of her the last year."

She pulled her hand away. "That must have been hard."

He nodded. "It wears you down, emotionally and physically. Her death was almost a…"

"A relief?"

He met her gaze and frowned. "That sounds horrible, but yes, in a way it was."

"No, not really. She isn't hurting any more. In a way she's free."

He smiled at her. She was right. That was exactly how he felt. He never talked about it to anyone, because he was afraid that they would judge him. That they would think he was a uncaring and selfish bastard. "Becca is free."

Danica offered a smile, then asked, "What do you do?"

"I'm a psychiatrist. Started my own practice after Becca died." He studied her as she poured syrup over her pancakes. She was the most exotic looking woman he'd ever seen. Tiny ribbons of reddish-blond hair left loose to frame her face teased him to touch them. Talking about Becca to her eased some of hurt he'd buried. "What about you?"

Her lashes lifted, revealing green irises. "I…was a heal…um, doctor."

"Was?"

She nodded. "My sense of touch in my right hand isn't what it used to be."

"Surly, there are other things you can do and still practice."

"That part of my life is over." When he opened his mouth to speak, she held a hand up. "We should hurry. Blaine will want us there early so he can torture you before feeding you."

He chuckled, catching the humor in her tone and the smile in her eyes. There was something captivating about this woman. He was determined to find out what.

THE RESIDENTS of Ashwood Falls buzzed around busy with preparations for the Winter Solstice festival. Danica parked the snowmobile in a small lot next to the community center and watched some leopard and wolf cubs throwing snowballs at each other. Nevan pulled up next to her and took off his helmet.

"They look like they're having fun."

She glanced at his face and then at his hands. "Don't you dare."

He waggled his brows. "I'll give you a head start."

Shit. He was seriously going to throw a snowball at her. She took off toward the park where the kids where playing, figuring she'd at least be a little safe. A solid ball of snow hit her in the back. She squealed, and the kids laughed.

"Oh, yeah?" She gathered some snow in her hands

to form a small ball. The children scattered as she threw it. It hit one of the Russell twins in the bottom. The six-year-old yelped playfully, and he fell to the ground as if he'd been shot, landing in the snow on his back with his arms spread out straight from his little body. Danica laughed, and then she let out a yelp when the sting of a frozen ball hit her on the butt.

Whirling around, she quickly picked up more snow to form an adult-sized ball and hurled it at Nevan, hitting him in the chest. He fell to the ground, and fear shot through her. Shit. She forgotten to hold back. Rushing over to him, she checked for a pulse, and she hovered her left hand over his chest.

Suddenly, she was pulled down and flipped onto her back, Nevan's smiling face inches from hers. "Gotcha," he said.

The rapid beats of her heart quickened to heavy thumps behind her ribcage at the thought of his lips touching hers. His pine-and-sage scent teased her muted sense of smell. He inched closer until a shadow fell over them.

They quickly stood to face the newcomer, and her happy mood turned sour. "Hello, Jared."

"Good morning, Dani." The alpha jaguar was dressed in his usual dress pants and button-up shirt underneath his black, unbuttoned wool jacket. Jared was very handsome with his sun-lightened brown hair and golden-brown eyes. He was the Packs' legal advisor; a lawyer by human definition. He aided Keegan and Luna—the wolf's Alpha female—in any, and all, legal issues that concerned the citizens of Ashwood Falls. He would be the perfect mate. But, Danica couldn't find the spark. Her cat wanted nothing to do with him.

"Who's your friend?"

Danica winced at the sharp undertone of his question. *Please, don't let him cause a scene. Not in front of the children.* Taking a breath, she linked the fingers of her scarred hand with Nevan's. "This is Nevan. Nevan, Jared."

Squeezing her hand slightly, Nevan nodded. "Nice to meet you." He held out his free hand to the cat.

Ignoring the offer, Jared met her stare. "I take it you're on your way to see Keegan."

"Yes. Blaine and Shay invited us over for a late lunch."

Jared narrowed his eyes, and his nostril flared a fraction. "I see."

A rain of snowballs assailed them, followed by children's laughter. Jared's face reddened with irritation, only making the twins, and leaders of the assault, increase the number of projectiles flying toward the well-dressed lawyer.

"Kyle! Cole!"

Danica turned to see Jasmine Russell, the twins' guardian and older sister, running at them, horror and fury in her expression.

"So sorry, Jared." She stopped between the boys and grabbed them by the upper arms.

Jared didn't comment. He just stormed off without a word.

Jasmine frowned. "Sorry. These two are always causing some kind of trouble." She held out her hand to Nevan. "Hi. Welcome to Ashwood Falls. I'm Jasmine."

Nevan shook her hand and smiled. "Thanks."

Jasmine excused herself and moved to march the boys home. Danica placed a hand on her arm, making her peer at her. "Don't be too hard on them. I found it very amusing."

Jasmine offered a weak smile and turned to leave.

"Come on. We should get going."

They walked down the sidewalk in silence. Nevan's scent was heavy with anxiety. And, she was going to feed him to the leopards. She wondered what was going through his mind. He had to have a thousand questions. He was a psychiatrist, trained to read and understand human behaviors. Had he picked up on Jared's animal-like presence?

"Look, I'm sorry about Jared. He's usually not so rude."

"He was jealous."

She stopped and faced him. "Really?"

He chuckled. "It's a human emotion everyone has. He obviously likes you and didn't like it that we were together. I'm a stranger, and he feels threatened."

Raising a brow, she studied him. "You're that good at reading people?"

He leaned into her and whispered, "I'm empathic."

Her breath hitched. How was that possible? She'd never heard of humans with the ability. Did he have shifter blood in his veins?

"There you two are."

Shay's chipper voice broke her from the swirl of questions in her mind.

The tigress continued her rapid speech in her care-free way. "Blaine has been running a groove in the floor. You know how he gets, Dani." She smiled at Nevan. "Morning! You're even cuter in natural light."

Danica released a growl before she could stop it. Shay peered at her, shocked and amused. "Sorry, my dear friend and sister." Shay looped her arms with

Danica's and laid her head on her shoulder. *"He's not for me."*

Smiling at the telepathic acknowledgment, Danica relaxed. A little. What unnerved her was the reaction she had because Shay gave Nevan a compliment. Damn. She was in so much trouble.

3

It had been the strangest twenty-four hours in Nevan's life. Well, at least stranger than it had been in the last five years. Growing up with four mountain lion-shifters would be pretty strange to the normal human.

However, the residents of this small town didn't seem too human. Then again, it could have been his imagination running wild. His hormones sure were on overdrive since he'd met Danica. Watching her smile at Shayna made him want to touch her, to see if her skin really was as creamy as it looked.

Shaking off the inappropriate thoughts, he followed the women into the house.

The large man from the night before was the first to greet them. The sense of familiarity settled over him again. He'd seen him somewhere before but could not place the where or when.

"Blaine. Relax."

Nevan cut his eyes toward the commanding voice. An older, larger man who looked a lot like Blaine entered the living room. His dark brown hair back in a loose ponytail, and his brown eyes darkened as he locked gazes with Nevan.

Danica linked her fingers with his and tugged him farther in the large living room. They stopped a couple of feet from the man. The only way Nevan thought to describe him was an alpha male. The energy flowing off him was similar to his oldest brother. Sarah had said his brother could be alpha of his own pack one day.

"I'm Keegan." He narrowed his dark brown eyes at Nevan and motioned to the couch. "Please have a seat. Lunch will be ready soon."

He felt like a hormonal teen meeting his date's father, but he fell into step with Danica as she led the way to the sofa. Even Danica seemed tense.

Keegan sat in a recliner across from them while Shay perched on the couch arm beside Danica and Blaine held the wall in place behind his father. "Blaine failed to get your last name."

Was he for real? The only thing Nevan wanted

was to call Sarah and let her know he was at least alive and maybe put a call out to the supernatural police or something. Because there was definitely something preternatural going on.

"My name is Nevan Mathews."

One of the alpha male's dark brows rose and amusement brightened his features. "Was your father Walt Mathews?"

Nevan cut his eyes to Blaine, who pushed away from the wall and studied him closer. *Like a bug under a microscope...* "Yes," he answered Keegan, meeting his gaze once more.

A frown wrinkled his forehead, and he tossed a cordless phone to Nevan. "Call Sarah and tell her I send my best." He stood, motioned to his son, and they left the room.

Confused, Nevan glanced at Danica. A wash of relief, happiness, and worry flowed from her. "I'll give you some privacy." She moved to stand, but he covered her hand.

"Stay."

She gave a short nod and sat back. Shay smiled at him and picked up Danica's right arm to gently massage her fingers and palm. Stopping the questions from tumbling out of his mouth, he dialed Sarah's number and wasn't surprised she answered after the first ring.

"Nev?"

"Yes, Ma. I'm fine."

"What happened? Where the hell are you?"

Closing his eyes, he took deep breaths to hold the buried pain in check. Hearing his stepmother's voice brought a flood of memories. Memories of his father and the family they'd once been. "I had an accident, but I'm not hurt."

"Where are you?"

"Ashwood Falls."

Silence filled the line for several seconds before she responded. "Are they…Have you met Keegan?"

He counted to three in his mind. She knew these people, knew of this town, yet, she'd never once mentioned it to him. Nor had his brothers ever spoken of it. All his life she'd taught him about the shifter way of life and the importance of secrecy. Was that it? She didn't trust him to keep the mountain town a secret?

"Yes, I met him, and he sends his best." He didn't keep the hurt out of his tone.

A soft sigh rushed through the phone. "The town is not of my people. It was not my secret to tell. Please don't be angry."

"What do you mean?"

"Please trust me. I can't spill secrets of another pack."

Pack? Was she serious? "I'm not understanding."

Danica's hand touched his knee, causing him to jump. Locking gazes, she whispered, "I'll explain later." The plea in her eyes made him want to hold her.

The annoyance drained from his body. "I'm sorry, Ma."

"I know, baby. You're one of my cubs, even if you can't shift."

That made him laugh. "Yeah, because I'm human."

"Shh. We won't talk about that," she teased. "Look, the little bit of snow we got last night was only the start of the huge storm headed this way. Stay there until it passes."

The way she could sense the weather change had always amazed him. "All right. Do you have everything you need?"

"Yes, Nev. We'll be fine. I have my grandbabies."

"What? Who?"

"Cale and Monica had a set of twins a couple of months ago. I thought I told you."

He sighed. "Oh, yes, I'd almost forgotten Cale

and Monica's twins." He'd been busy forgetting and burying his pain.

"Don't worry about it. You'll get to meet your nieces soon."

He smiled and glanced at the females at the end of the couch, cuddled up like the pair of cats, listening to the conversation. Everything fell into place. The too-careful actions of everyone around him and the over protectiveness Blaine had shown the night before made sense. "I'll see you when the storm passes. Love you, Mama."

A choked sob came from Sarah before she responded. "It's been too long since you called me that. Love you, too."

Swallowing the lump in his throat, he disconnected the call and peered at Danica and Shay. Both women looked back at him as though they were about to cry. "What's wrong?"

Danica smiled. "You called her mama. That's so sweet."

"And girly."

Nevan clenched his jaw at the sound of Blaine's voice. Before he could lash back, Shay reached out and hit the large shifter in the stomach hard enough that he took a step back. "Shut it, Blaine."

A few seconds later, Shay squealed as he flipped

her over his shoulder. The smile on his face read of the pure love a brother would have for his sister. "Watch it, kitty, or I'll rearrange your potions, again."

She kicked wildly. "Don't you dare, leopard-boy!"

"Leopard?" Nevan studied Danica as she stiffened then dropped her shoulders.

"It was me. I'm the reason you're stuck here instead of being with your family."

Her guilt rushed out to him. "It was an accident." He knew from his brothers that, when in animal form, they thought like the animal. The headlights mostly likely had startled her. "I was tired and not concentrating on the road."

"But, your car."

He chuckled. "It's a rental, and I bought insurance."

She laughed at his poor excuse of a joke and reach out to touch his cheek. Her pale green eyes brightened and seemed to dance. His gaze lowered to her lower lip she held between her teeth. Suddenly, he had the urge to kiss her. Keegan's husky tone calling them to the dining room broke them from whatever trance they'd fallen under. Much too quickly, she stood and rushed away. All he could do was watch her follow her family into the other room.

Get a grip, Nev.

BACK AT THE CABIN, alone with Nevan, Danica thought she'd be more relaxed now that he knew what she was, but she'd been wrong. Her cat was hyper-aware of every movement and the heat of his stare. The more time she spent with him, the more intrigued she became.

To try to shake off some of the rising need, she turned toward the fireplace. Nevan stepped in her path and touched her lightly on the hand. Sparks of desire rippled on her skin, and startled her.

"What is it?"

She peered into his gray-blue eyes and smiled. "I felt that."

"My touch?"

She laughed at the confusion that passed over his face. "My right hand…I usually don't feel the light weight of others' fingers. It must be working." She turned toward the kitchen.

"What's working?"

She lifted her head to peer at him across the island countertop. "Shay. She has…" She sucked her lip between her teeth, unsure of how much to tell him. However, he did have mountain lion shifters as his mother and four stepbrothers. He was already aware of their world. "She has a small amount of magick in her blood."

He didn't flinch or seemed a bit surprised at the news. She relaxed, but only a tiny bit.

"Is she part witch?"

She shook her head. "I don't think so. It isn't uncommon for shifters to possess magickal abilities. Blaine can teleport. Keegan is telepathic."

"Oh, great. I'll have to remember that. Sarah and my brothers don't have any special gifts."

"Not all weres have them. Some theories are that certain blood lines carry magick from the early ancestors." She withdrew two stemless wine glasses from the cupboard. "Do you like red wine?"

His smile reached his eyes for the first time since he'd been there, and she had to press her hands on the counter to stay upright. "Yes."

It took her several seconds before she found her voice. "Can you start the fire?"

With a short nod, he moved to do as she requested. "So, what does Shay have to do with the feeling in your hand?"

"Oh. For the last couple of weeks, I've agreed to let her stimulate the nerves in my right hand and arm." After pouring the wine and returning the bottle to the mini-fridge, she carried both glasses to the living room.

"That's what she was doing earlier? Before lunch."

"She can send light currents of energy to my nerves by massaging my fingers and palm."

He ignited the oak, and when satisfied with the flame, he returned the screen and faced her. "And, it's helping?"

She smiled, handing him a glass. "It appears so." She sat down on the sofa with one leg tucked under her.

He sat next to her. "How much can you tell me about Ashwood Falls? Sarah said to ask Keegan. I gathered from her tone it's a Pack secret or something."

"The lions had a treaty with our pack centuries ago. They are bound from speaking about the town or who lives here. Although, I'm not sure why she wouldn't tell you since you're her family."

He looked out the glass door that overlooked the backyard. "She broke from her pack a couple of years before mating with my father. None of us kids know why. Or, if the others do, they've been forbidden to talk about it."

"Oh. Some packs are more secretive than others. I don't know much about the lions."

He chuckled. "That makes two of us."

She took a sip of her wine before speaking. "Ashwood Falls was formed on the land of two Packs: the wolves and the leopards. Both Packs lost over sixty percent of their people during a mass attack from a rogue shifter pack called the Onyx."

Nevan made a noise of disgust. "How long ago?"

"It was over two hundred years ago. They came in like a storm. The weaker of the Packs surrendered and now work with the Onyx for their cause."

He raised a brow. "You don't know what that is, do you?"

"No. I suspect the Enforcers have some leads or an idea. The given is they want control over all packs and territories." Visions of the night she lost her parents came to mind. Her throat tightened and she fought to keep the tears from falling. Even after all these years, she still could recall their memories without crying. "I lost my parents in that attack."

He twisted his body to sit sideway on the sofa and faced her. "Sorry."

"I was ten years old at the time. My mom tucked me inside a hidden room in the basement. I heard everything.

Their screams, the breaking glass, shouts from the rogues to kill everyone…" Lifting her gaze, she met Nevan's gray stare. Fury darkened his eye color to the color of storm clouds. "Blaine found me. At the time it seemed like days. I already knew my parents were dead."

Nodding, he reached over and covered her hand. "Sarah cried out in pain when my dad died. She felt the loss, and my brothers felt hers. I had no clue what was going on until they told me. It was the first time I ever felt like an outsider."

She curled her fingers around his hand and squeezed. "They never meant…"

He peered at her, holding her completely captive.

"I know. But I had to leave after that. With Dad, everything was whole. We were family. We still are, but we're missing a piece."

The crackling from the fire filled the room. She understood what he described. The bond between Sarah and her mate being broken would have been painful. Keegan, in one of his very rare emotional moods, had described it to her. The Alpha had said it was as if someone had reached inside his chest and ripped his heart out with their bare hands. She figured it would be rude and inappropriate to ask how he knew what that felt like and considered he was being graphic to keep her from asking any more personal questions.

When she looked up again, it was to meet Nevan's eyes. Desire swirled in them, awakening her leopard. He raised his hand to brush a stray hair from her face. Instead of dropping his hand, he slid it behind her neck and drew her closer. His earthy pine scent enveloped her. When his lips touched hers, she lost any hope of control.

She opened, allowing his tongue inside to dance with hers. Her skin tingled and warmed at the pleasure that consumed her. It'd been way too long since she had been kissed like this. Never in her two hundred twenty-three years of life did she remember a kiss being this good.

His fingers touched her belly, making her jump slightly. When his palm cupped her breast, she moaned and pressed into his touch. Then he brushed over a path of scars, and she stilled.

Palms flat on his chest, she gave a gentle push. He broke the kiss. "What…?"

Shaking, she said, "I can't," and ran out the back door with her inhuman speed.

4

———————

*D*anica fell to her knees in the snow about twenty yards from the cabin, her flesh still heated from Nevan's kiss and the way he'd moved his hand over her skin. The need to bite him and claim him as hers had made her run away from him. Then there were the scars and the fear he would reject her after he saw how much of her body was ruined.

A tear dropped, forming a dent in the snow. She had spent the last couple of years living alone and coming to terms with the idea of never finding a mate. And she'd just run away from a potential mate. God, she was an idiot.

"Dani?"

Her head snapped up at Jared's questioning tone.

Great. She didn't need him, or anyone, seeing her like this. "What do you want?"

"I came to talk to you. Why are you out here?" He paused and sniffed the air. "I see."

She stood and brushed off her jeans. "See what?"

"I petitioned Keegan for your hand."

Choking, she squeaked, "You did what?"

Extending his hand to caress her cheek, he grew more serious than she'd ever seen him. "You need someone to care for you, to provide you with the security you deserve."

She swatted at his hand. "You don't love me, and I'm not entering a loveless mating."

"We're friends, Dani. We could grow to love each other over time. My parents' mating was arranged, as was your parents', and they loved one another deeply."

"My parents were in love from the day they met." She whirled around, only to have him stop her with his hand wrapped around her bicep.

"I can give you everything you desire."

Squaring her shoulders, she pulled free from his hold and locked gazes with him. "Could you ever make love to me with the lights on? Could you look at my scars without flinching? Without pity?"

His silence confirmed his answer. "I didn't think so."

He stepped closer to her and drew her into a hug. "I've seen the scars."

Another tear rolled down her cheek. Yes, Jared had seen her after the fire and had been there, with Shay, during the painful healing. "You still look at me with sorrow. I don't want people to dwell on those feelings anymore."

He lifted her chin with his finger. "You don't have to give me your answer now. Think about it."

Stepping back, he moved his gaze past her before he shifted into a large jaguar and vanished deeper into the forest.

"Dani, what's going on?"

She closed her eyes briefly before turning to face Nevan. Gut turning, she hated that hurt look on his face. "How long have you been here?"

"Long enough." He stood staring at her for several moments before speaking again. "I'm just going to leave. It was a mistake to agree to stay with you."

He pivoted around and marched back to the cabin. Cursing, she rushed after him. "Where will you go? It's about to snow again. You'll freeze…"

Stopping at the bottom step, he spoke without looking at her. "I'll go into town and call my brother."

Fear squeezed her heart. If he left, she'd never see him again. He could be her one, and maybe only, chance at have a true mate, and he was about to walk out of her life. He couldn't leave, not now. "Don't go. Please." He shook his head and continued up the stairs and into the house. She followed him down the hall to the guest room. When she entered the room, her fear turned to nervous desperation to keep him.

"You can't leave."

He looked at her then. "I can't?"

Her legs started to shake. She'd gone too long avoiding the male species; she wasn't sure what to do. "I just found you. I can't let you leave," she whispered.

Standing stock-still, he studied her. "Who is Jared, really?"

Taking a shaky breath, she wrapped her arms around her middle. "He's Ashwood Falls' legal counsel."

He stepped into her space, making her heart rate increase. "No, who is he to you?"

"A close friend. That's it. He's not my true mate."

"Have you two ever…?"

"No."

His expression hardened a little. "I heard him say he'd seen your scars."

With a sigh, she sat on the bed. "Jared pulled me out of the fire and was there through my recovery."

"Sounds like more than a friend."

She focused back on his face. Her own fury started to rise. "Jared has a problem with thinking he knows what's best for others. He also is known for chasing after weaker females."

"You're not weak." He stalked toward her. The gleam in those grey eyes sent heat to her sex. "What did you mean by finding me and not letting me go?"

She swallowed. "I…you're the one who's my potential true mate."

He stopped a couple of inches from her and cupped her face. She covered his hand with hers and watched shock, confusion, and hint of joy pass over his handsome features in a swirl of emotion. He opened his mouth to speak, but closed it.

She kissed his palm, stopping him from saying anything. Peering up at him through her thick lashes, she drew his index finger into her mouth. His sharp intake of breath and the increase in his pulse encouraged her to continue. She ran her hand up the inside of his leg, stopping inches below the growing bulge behind his zipper.

His fingers wrapped around hers and pulled her hand away. With their gazes locked, he withdrew his finger from her mouth so he could cup the back of her head. She watched the play of emotions on his face. There was a battle going on inside his mind.

"Relax, Doctor. Do what you want and stop analyzing the situation," she challenged.

His gray eyes darkened as his scent intensified. He lowered his head to capture her lips. Like the first one had, this kiss ignited her from the inside out. She moaned and pressed into him, offering herself to him. What they both needed.

The internal debate was over. Maybe it was overridden by desire. Whatever the case, Danica didn't care. He broke the kiss, drew back, and lifted the hem of her sweater.

A rush of fear shot through her, increasing her pulse and threatening to close off her airway. Pushing the garment back down, she was beginning to have a panic attack. "Turn the lights off."

He stopped all movement and made eye contact. "No."

She shook her head and tried to calm the raging fear. "I can't…don't want…"

With a sigh, he sat next to her and linked his fingers with hers. "I've seen burns before. Many of them far worse than yours."

The anxiety eased and she looked away, embarrassed. He cupped her cheek, drawing her attention back to him. "I volunteer with the children's burn unit at my local hospital. I learned quickly that the last thing those kids need is pity."

She searched his face. "No one's seen the scars besides Shay, Cameron, and Jared."

A tic formed in his temple at the mention of Jared's name. Her cat liked the spark of jealousy. "Who's Cameron?"

"She's one of the female Enforcers and Shay's best friend."

He smiled, sparking the desire up again. Her heart thumped irregularly, and she swallowed as he shifted closer. "If I *am* your true mate, then you'll need to trust I won't run at the sight of your body."

Damn. She wasn't sure she could do it. Yes, moments ago, she'd been ready to claim him and had needed him inside her; she still did. But, the fear of rejection had taken over and turned her chicken. However, he had a point. She was sure he was her mate, and she had to trust the Fates knew what they were doing.

Closing her eyes, she removed her sweater and waited. There was no change in his breathing, no change in his scent, indicating his disgust. Slowly she opened her eyes to find Nevan's desire-filled gaze surveying her like a delicacy. Her body heated, and for the first time since the accident, she felt desired, wanted, and beautiful.

"You're beautiful."

She was about to protest when his mouth covered hers in a searing kiss that sent tiny pricks of sensation through her body. When his tongue dipped inside her mouth seeking hers, she released a soft moan. She trailed her fingers down his side to the hem of his shirt and tugged. He broke the kiss to remove the garment.

Dear. God.

He was build like a cat, full of lean muscle and yummy. Licking her lips, she placed her palm on his chest and threaded her fingers through the dust of blond hair. He pressed into her, forcing her to lie back. When her back touched the mattress, he lifted from her and proceeded to remove her pants.

She sat back up, holding on to his wrist. "Wait." Her heart hammered behind her ribs.

He pressed a quick kiss to her lips. "Do the scars get worse?"

She shook her head. "No."

"Then lie back like a good kitty."

A smile stretched her lips at his teasing. "And if I misbehave?"

"Then I'll have to punish you."

The sexy smirk and erotic tone in which he spoke sent a tidal wave of desire through her. "You wouldn't."

He leaned in and pressed his lips to her cheek. "Try me."

Yes. That was a challenge. Her cat meowed in her mind, begging for her to push him. Laughing, she wrapped her legs around his waist and drew him to her as she bit gently on his ear lobe.

He hissed and rocked his hips into her. "You like to bite?"

"I'm a cat, aren't I?"

She chuckled as he rose to settle on his knees between her thighs. She watched him slide down her legs, then slowly tug her pants off and toss them to the floor. The urge to cover herself weighed heavy on her, but she pushed it away. Nevan looked at her with hunger in his eyes as though her skin was perfect.

Starting at her ankle, he trailed light kisses up her right side, being sure to pay attention to each imperfect, ugly patch of skin. The burns didn't cover everywhere. They were a spatter of scarred patches left from what her natural healing powers couldn't fix. It was enough to disfigure her and make lovers pity her.

That was why she'd decided to live in the cabin and never take a mate.

Nevan was different. There was no pity in his lust-drunken gaze. "What is it?"

Smiling, she reached out and cupped his face. "You make me feel."

He turned his head so his lips touched her palm. "I'm not usually like this. I mean I don't sleep with women I just met."

She frowned. "I never thought…"

"I know. I just wanted you to know. I haven't been with anyone since Becca."

With a finger pressed to his lips, she tried to soothe him. "Shh." She sat up and kissed his lips. "It's okay."

She moved her legs from around him, but he stopped her. "Don't leave."

Studying him, she could see the conflict in his features and feel his desire in his touch. God, she was so out of practice reading people. "Tell me what you need from me." She'd do anything for him. She wanted nothing more than to possess his body and mark him as hers, but she understood grief. She'd dealt with it personally when she lost her parents and had seen it nearly destroy Keegan when he lost his mate.

"Everyone in Ashwood's been touched with loss in one form or another. That's what makes us such a tight community."

He peered at her and nodded. "I felt that today. The love and friendship that linger in the air like magick."

"That's the bond between the packs."

Silence filled the room for several moments before he picked her hand and linked his fingers with hers. "I'm not sure what I need, but I know I want you."

"And, that makes you feel guilty." After his nod, she continued. "I'm a very patient kitty." She shifted closer to him. "And, skilled in stalking my prey."

She squeaked when he tackled her to the bed. "You make me feel, too." He captured her lips in a deep, passionate kiss.

Threading her fingers through his hair, she drew him closer. She opened her mouth for his tongue. Once it slipped inside she sucked on it, pulling a groan from him. She smiled and released his tongue and moved her lips across his cheek to his ear. "Lose the jeans," she purred, then gently bit his earlobe.

He shuttered and lifted his head to lock gazes with her. His gray eyes reminded her of storm clouds, and they were full of passion.

Yet, he hesitated. "I don't have a condom."

She smiled. "I'm not in heat, and I'm immune to human diseases." She cupped his head and tugged him down for a hard, passionate kiss. Pulling away, she peered into his eyes. "Nor can I pass anything onto you."

He kissed her on the nose, stood, and removed his clothes. Danica drank in the sight of him. Oh, God, it had been way too long. She sat up, rose from the bed and lowered to her knees in front of him. Peering up into his face, she ran a hand up his thigh to his thick cock. She wrapped her fingers around it and stroked. Nevan closed his eye and sank his fingers in her hair. She moaned as he lightly tugged the hand full of hair.

When she took him into her mouth, she felt his leg muscles tighten under her touch. He pulled on her hair again, but this time it was to stop her. She released him, and he took her upper arms and pulled her to a stand.

She protested, "I wasn't done."

He shook his head. "If you didn't stop, I would be."

Giggling, she kissed his lips. "But we would have make up for it in the second round."

She pushed him down on the bed. As if knowing what she wanted, he laid back and waited. She climbed up on the bed and straddled him. His cock throbbed as she took it in her hand, the large vein hot under her touch. She let out a moan as she guided him to her pussy, then lowered herself on to him, his thickness stretching her in the best way possible.

He grasped her hips, his fingers biting into her skin as she rode him until they screamed out in release.

5

Unsure what had woken him, Nevan couldn't shake the uneasiness settling into his chest. Something was off. He lay wide eye on his back and listened to his surroundings. His brothers had taught him to slow his breathing and focus on the space around him. Very few humans were sensitive enough to notice the changes in air pressure and sounds. Nevan was one of the few.

The house was quiet, too quiet. He sat up in bed, noticing that Danica was gone. He flung the covers off, pulled on his jeans, and rushed across the hall to her room. She wasn't there. He turned then ran down the hall and stopped at the foyer. Panic started to build, tightening his chest. Her boots sat by the door and her coat hung on the hook a few feet away.

Had she gone hunting? Maybe, but the lingering dread that woke him still said something had happened.

The front door flew open, and Nevan found himself face-to-face with a female shifter dressed in black jeans and a leather jacket. Her aggression rolled off her in thick, threatening waves.

Pure adrenaline and protectiveness pushed him forward to grab the woman by the neck and flatten her against the wall. Pressing into her small frame so she couldn't move, he growled, "You're not a leopard. Who are you, and where the hell is Dani?"

She raised a brow and smirked. "If you don't want every bone in your body broken, you'll release me, human."

"Not until you tell me where Dani is."

In a matter of seconds, Nevan's face was pressed against the wall with the hand he'd had around the female's neck twisted behind his back. She leaned in with her full weight and whispered, "You have balls. Why the hell do you think I'm here?"

"Cameron, let go of the human. Danica will be pissed if you harm him."

Nevan recognized the male voice as Keegan's. The female released him and disappeared to explore the house. Nevan flexed his wrist and peered at Keegan. "Who the hell is that?"

The Alpha's lips twitched. "One of my best Enforcers."

"No shit." He jerked his gaze to the door as Blaine came in with an expression that told Nevan the Enforcer was ready to kill.

"Her scent is too faint." Turning those gray eyes toward Nevan, Blaine growled, "She's been gone for at least two hours."

"What? Can't be." How had she left the house without him knowing? Because he was human. Damn it.

Frowning, Cameron came back into the room. "She left in cat form."

"How do you know that?" Nevan glared at the female.

"Boots are at the door, coat on the hangers, and her clothes are on the floor in the guest room."

Blaine flashed to stand in front of her, swiped her dark hair from her shoulders, then shifted toward Nevan. "You touched her."

"Dani? That's none of your business."

Keegan stepped in front of his son and growled, "Leave it," then walked out the door. Blaine followed. Cameron rolled her eyes and gestured for him to go first. He grabbed his jacket and put his shoes on as he stepped out in the cold.

When Cameron stepped in line with Nevan, he asked, "What kind of cat are you?"

"What makes you think I'm a cat?"

Nevan snorted. "I lived most my life with lions. You move like a cat."

Blaine growled again. Cameron growled back, and Nevan couldn't help but wonder what the story was with the two of them.

"Black jaguar."

"Oh, like Jared."

She sighed. "Jared is my brother."

Her don't-ask tone told him to shut his mouth. Plus Blaine's growls turned to snarls, and he inched closer to them with each question.

Several yards into the woods, Keegan stopped and held his hand up. Blaine cursed. "She's bleeding."

Nevan's heart rate kicked into overdrive. She was hurt. He couldn't do anything. Just like he hadn't been able to protect Becca from her illness. He moved up to stand by the two alpha males. "What do you mean?"

As soon as the questions tumbled out of his mouth, he felt it—a pull to something deeper in the forest. He started walking toward it then jogged when he felt the hint of pain that his empathic ability picked up.

He skidded to a halt at the sight of a leopard tangled in barbwire. She had struggled and managed to get some of the wire embedded in her skin. Nevan stepped forward, she growled. Her breath was labored, and her pain gripped him. The snow around here was colored red with her blood. Blaine advanced, ignoring the snaps of her teeth.

"Come on, sissy. I need to get you untangled." She snapped at him again, catching him on the hand. He cursed and jerked back. "Cam."

Cam pulled a pistol out of her thigh holster and aimed it at Danica.

Keegan's huge arms wrapped around Nevan before he could get to the jaguar. "It's a tranquilizer gun. Do you really think I'd kill my own?"

Nevan relaxed a little and shook his head.

The sound of the gun firing and the sight of Danica slipping into a restful sleep didn't ease any of his worry.

IT SEEMED to take Blaine forever to get Danica untangled from the barbs and back home. Nevan hadn't left her side in the two hours they'd been back. In the short expanse of one day, the leopard had found a way into his heart. Almost losing her was the wake-up call he'd needed.

"Why hasn't she shifted by now?"

Shay met his gaze and offered a tender smile. "The tranq they gave her will keep her in leopard form. She can heal faster this way."

That made sense. He reached out to stroke her fur but withdrew his hand before it made a connection.

"You won't hurt her. The worst has healed."

Watching Danica's side rise and fall as she slept, he shrugged. "Does it always happen this fast?" When she didn't answer, he turned and noticed her perplexed expression. "The mating."

Color rose in her cheeks and she turned her head. "I don't know. I'm twenty-five, and I'm a baby, according to my brothers and father. They don't let me far from their sight." She rolled her eyes and put aside the bowl with the creamy concoction she'd brought with her. "But, I've seen some mates meet and bond in the same day. I've been told that you just know when you meet the one you belong with. Cam and Blaine have been doing the mating dance since she came of age."

"Came of age?"

She stood and moved to the window. Nevan was about to tell her never mind, that he hadn't meant to embarrass her, when she answered the question. "It's when a female shifter enters her first heat cycle."

"And you haven't?" When she shook her head and didn't look at him, he cursed. "Sorry, that was too personal."

"Oh, no. It's okay. I'm just a late bloomer. Most females go through their first cycle by their twenty-third birthday." She fell silent and peered at the door.

A few seconds later, the door opened slowly, and Jared stepped into the room. Nevan suppressed a groan and nodded at the male in greeting. Jared gave a sharp nod back and asked, "How is she? How did this happen?"

Shay narrowed her eyes at him. "Blaine thinks it was poachers setting up traps."

"It's too close to home. What are the Enforcers doing?"

"We're doing our job." Cameron spoke from the open door. "Stop being an ass, Jared."

"All right. Dani needs her rest." Shay pushed away from the window and shooed everyone out. She sent Nevan a wink before she shut the door with a soft click.

Silence filled the bedroom. Movement on the bed

startled him. Turning to check on Danica, he gasped at her naked, lean body stretching. His erotic, beautiful shifter.

She smiled and placed her palm against his cheek. "I thought they'd never leave."

He raised a brow. "How long have you been awake?"

"Long enough to hear about coming of age." She laughed and growled as if in pain.

He jumped up on his knees to hover over her. "What is it?"

"Just bruising." When she lifted her lids to meet his disbelieving stare, she took a deep breath. Nevan held in his smile, knowing she was trying not the laugh. "Honest. It hurts to laugh."

He frowned and caressed her cheek with the backs of his fingers. "Why did you go outside? I mean how did you get caught in the wire?"

She sighed. "I heard something. It's not uncommon for humans to set up camp in the woods near here. Even in this weather. Crazy humans. So I changed into a leopard and went out to scare off whatever it was. I walked right into the barbwire. It was never there before. This is Ashwood land. There shouldn't have been a fence there."

Wanting to easy her growing distress, he bent

down and kissed her forehead. "I'll go warm up the soup Shay brought."

She stopped him with a palm on his chest. "I'm not hungry."

"She said it would help."

"It will help me sleep. I don't want to sleep."

His cock perked up at her provocative tone and the desire in her gaze. She couldn't mean…

She pressed her index finger on his lips. "Stop thinking."

He opened his mouth and took her finger inside with his tongue. Her sharp intake of breath enticed him to take what he wanted. Screw logic and screw his analytical mind that felt it was necessary to find reason in everything he did. It'd been too long since he had enjoyed the touch of another. The longer he was near Danica, the stronger the urge became.

"Are you sure you're healed enough?"

She raised the brows, and her mouth curved into a seductive smile. "Are *you* sure?"

Was he ever? It was time to move on. His time with Becca had been wonderful, and he still loved her, but he'd never felt the way he did with Danica. For the first time in years, he felt he had a future waiting for him. "Yes. I can't not have you."

"Good." She cupped his head and drew him in for a kiss.

Nevan deepened the kiss. He trailed his hand down her side to her thigh and lifted so her leg wrapped around his. She let out a soft moan that sounded more like a purr.

She tugged his shirt up and slid her hand underneath. Nevan gasped and jerked. "Your hands are cold," he said against her lips.

Giggling, she slipped her other one under the shirt. "Then warm them."

"You like being a naughty kitty?"

She raised her head and bit his earlobe. "Yes."

He stood, putting distance between them before he came in his jeans. Danica was an erotic beauty lying on her back, bare, with desire in her eyes. She cupped her left breast and rolled the nipple between her fingers. His dick pressed harder into the zipper of his pants. Without releasing his stare, she moved her other hand down her stomach to slip her fingers between the folds of her pussy.

He was sure she was torturing him. He ripped the shirt over his head and removed his pants. She let out a soft cry of pleasure. Nevan took her wrist and lifted her fingers to his mouth. A sharp intake of breath escaped her when he sucked on her fingers. He met her green-eyed stare, now heavy with desire, and moved to kneel between her legs.

Leaning forward, he placed a kiss on her belly and trailed light kisses down to her inner thigh where he bit lightly. She whimpered and sank her fingers into his hair to grip a handful. He lifted his head to peer into her passion-filled eyes and held her stare as he licked her clit. Her leg shook, and he felt her mounting pleasure as well as his own. He snaked two fingers through her slick folds then entered her while continuing to stroke her clit with his thumb. Another cry of pleasure escaped her. He picked up his tempo, increasing the building pleasure until an orgasm shook her body.

Nevan crawled up her body as another shudder left her body and positioned his cock at her entrance. Her dreamy-eyed green gaze locked with his and slowly slid inside her and groaned. She was so perfect, as though she'd been made for him. Wrapping her legs around his, Danica urged him closer. Her nails pierced the skin on his back. The sharp sting faded into a pleasure so intense it surged through his body like a current. He quickened his pace as Danica's pussy milked him until an orgasm tore through him at the same time Dani cried out with one of her own.

6

The afternoon sun shone through the blinds, casting streams of light across the floor. Danica stretched her pleasantly sore muscles. The things Nevan had done to her rolled around in her mind, rousing the hunger again. Damn, that man was fast becoming her addiction. She rolled over and frowned at the empty side of the bed. Wondering where he'd gone, she swung her legs over the side of the bed and peered at the clock. *Shit*. It was one in the afternoon.

She'd never slept in that late. Then again, she'd had the best sex of her life. A snicker tumbled from her lips, followed by a sigh at the smell of bacon on the air. Her stomach growled, pushing her into motion. Grabbing her robe, she secured it in place and went down the hall to the kitchen.

Entering the kitchen, she had to fight a moan. Nevan stood in front of the stove in nothing but jeans. She stepped up behind him and wrapped her arms around his waist. "Aren't you cold?"

He turned in her arms. "Nope. I've got the fire going and muffins in the oven."

"Mmm. They smell wonderful. Blueberry?"

He chuckled, slid his hands to her ass, and lifted her off the ground. She wrapped her legs around him. "Shay said they were your favorite."

She pulled back, confused. 'When did you talk to her?"

"She stopped by this morning to check on you."

Color rose in his cheeks, making her smile. "You can't hide scents from shifters."

He locked gazes with her. "No, you can't. But I think she was a little embarrassed, too."

"That's my baby sis."

"She brought by some more herbs for you."

"Oh, good. I'm about out."

He sat her on the counter and tended to the bacon in the skillet. "What are they for?"

"Tea. Some of them help with healing. Shay hopes that my scars will diminish over time." A pang in her heart caused her to look away from him, but his empathy kicked in, and he knew as soon as her mood changed.

He stepped into her line of sight and brushed the robe aside to press a tender kiss on her scarred breast. "They are part of you. I think you are beautiful with them."

"I'm not perfect like other shifters."

"I don't want perfect because it doesn't exist in any species."

Overwhelmed with emotion, she peered into his gray eyes and realized that she was falling in love with him. He accepted her for who she was and saw past the physical imperfections. He saw *her*. "Nevan. I—"

A knock on the door startled both of them. Nevan straightened her robe and helped her down so she could answer the door.

Dread flooded her system upon seeing Keegan and Jared on the front porch. "Keegan. Jared." She moved to the side to let them in.

The Alpha nodded to Nevan in greeting before speaking. "Dani, in light of the accident yesterday, I have given Jared my blessings to mate with you."

Her heart stopped, and her lungs refused to work for a moment. "No."

"It's done," Jared said and moved closer to her.

She jerked away from him. "I told you no. I don't want a loveless mating." She flicked her gaze to Keegan. "Are you forcing me into this? Is that your Alpha command?"

Keegan flinched at her harsh tone. She didn't care. This whole thing was wrong. She'd found her mate. She sought him out and found him standing against the counter, arms folded over his broad, bare chest. Something settled inside her, something close to fear, worried about what he was about to do or say.

Nevan pushed away from the counter and squared his shoulders. "I claim Danica as my mate."

Her mouth fell open. What? Joy, relief, and fear churned inside her belly. "You don't have to do this." What was she saying? She should be happy that he'd want to claim her, but she was so fearful of the outcome of such a challenge her belly felt like a million butterflies where trapped inside.

"Yes, I do." He stared at Keegan before continuing. "She told me I was her mate and…" He peered at her. "…I'm in love with her."

Keegan sighed. "I see. Dani, is this true?"

Trembling, she nodded. "Yes . He's my mate."

Jared fumed, "It's too late. He can't take care of

her. Look what happened yesterday. He didn't even know she'd left the cabin. And he's human."

His alpha male bullshit pissed Danica off. "That's bullshit, Jared! I've lived in this cabin for the last four years. By myself! And that human sees more than my scars." She got in his personal space and poked him in the chest. A low growl came from his throat. Nevan shifted beside them. "I love him, and I've already chosen. It's him. Not you."

A smirk lifted the corner of his lips. "I challenge him to a hunt."

"I accept," Nevan growled.

NEVAN COULD FEEL the fear rolling off Danica at his acceptance of the Hunt. He wanted to go to her, to comfort her and let her know that it would be okay. But that would only show weakness on his part in front of the males in front of him.

"Do you understand what you are getting into?"

Nevan met the Alpha's stare. "Yes."

The Hunt is a challenge of strength and wills. Nevan and Jared would hunt a single prey. His oldest brother, Cale, had told him once that most the time it was deer, because they are fast.

Jared gave a short nod. "Good. We begin at twilight." He turned and left.

Keegan moved toward the door then turned back. "You need more time?"

"No. I'll be ready."

Without another word, the Alpha walked out the door.

When Nevan turned toward Danica, he dropped his shoulders and held out his hand. She didn't take it. Instead, she glared at him with her lips pursed. "What are you doing? Jared is a very skilled hunter."

"And you don't think I am?"

She opened her mouth and closed it then whispered, "I don't know."

He took her hands and drew them in to rest over his heart. "Do you really believe my brothers went easy on me because I'm human?"

Her green gaze lightened. "No. They would have pushed you to your limits."

"And they got scolded by Momma every time."

She laughed. "I'll bet. Blaine and Alec still get in trouble for the shit they put Shay through. They call it training. Keegan wants to keep her under glass." She sighed and pressed her cheek to his chest. "I wish you would have let me challenge him."

He lifted her chin with a finger to peer into her

eyes. "I meant everything I said. I want to keep you, and if I have to win a Hunt to do it, then that's what I'm going to do."

She studied him closer, and he could almost hear the thoughts tumbling around in her head. Her eyes narrowed, and she smirked. "You've been on a Hunt before."

It wasn't a question, but a knowing on her part. Whether she sensed it or had just figured it out, she knew.

"My brothers and I went on Hunts. Cale said it was a way to hone into my empathic abilities. I can connect with nature as well as people's emotions." Before she could ask any more questions, he captured her lips in a hard, passionate kiss. She snaked her arms around his neck, pulling him closer. He scooped her up in his arms and carried her to the bedroom.

"This will be the only form of communication." Cameron's firm tone drew Nevan's gaze from Danica to the Enforcer handing a tiny earpiece to Jared. The large male rolled his eyes and put the device in his ear. Cameron glared at her brother. "I mean it. No mind linking. And no shifting."

Danica held an identical earpiece in front of Nevan's face. "Right or left?"

Nevan focused back on Danica's green gaze. He smiled and reached for it. She jerked it back, shaking her head. "Let me."

"Right." Shifting to allow her to secure the earpiece in place, he ran his fingers through her hair.

She shivered and locked gazes with him. "I still don't like this."

"It has to be done. I'll always be *the human* to them otherwise."

Her shoulders dropped. "I know." She leaned into him, pressing her breast against his chest. "But you're *my* human."

Snaking his arms around her, he captured her lips unconcerned of the others in the room until someone cleared their throat. They broke the kiss, and Danica stepped aside. Nevan gave her hand a light squeeze and moved toward the door.

He stepped out into the cold winter evening. *At least it's not snowing, again.* He drew in a deep breath, taking in the crisp, clean mountain air around him. The only sound was the tops of the trees swaying in the breeze. It was as though nature knew what was about to happen and waited for the show to begin.

Cameron and Blaine walked around him and down the stairs. Blaine looked toward the sky. "Cam and I will watch the south boundary; the wolves have the north."

Nevan walked down the stairs and took in the surrounding forest. The wolves Blaine spoke of were two more Enforcers, Hayden and Dane. Nevan had met them briefly when they arrived. For the first time, he'd sensed a tension between the males, but he brushed it off as being the difference between the wolves and cats. It was definitely going to be fun to witness how these different packs coexisted in one small town.

Jared stepped up beside him. In sync, they nodded and jogged off into the forest in different directions.

Nevan stopped several yards into the thick forest and listened, using his empathy to connect to the world around him. It was what gave him the edge and allowed him to meet his brothers head-on when they'd competed as teens. Apparently, he was one of the few humans sensitive to the energy levels around him. To people outside his paranormal family, he simple explained it as "just a feeling," but to his family, and now Danica, he was free to use his empathic gift to the fullest.

Kneeling down, he placed a palm against the base of a large oak. A light thumping vibration met his touch. The deer. He smiled, stood and cut left as soundlessly as he could.

When he came to a small clearing, he stilled and listened again. A sound too heavy to be a deer drew his attention to the left. Jared moved silently through the trees. Just then a deer darted into his sight. Crouching down, Nevan prepared to chase the animal.

But, the deer stopped, stood still as stone for a moment, and then one ear moved as if detecting something. Nevan remained crouched, trying not to make a sound.

Without warning, the deer took off. Jared ran after it. Cursing, Nevan chased them. Something was out there. "I'm picking up something. Do any of you see or hear anything?"

Blaine's voice came through the radio first. "Not where I am. Hayden?"

"Nope, all clear. Dane and I will split up."

"Jared?" Nevan prompted.

"Spooked, human?" Jared's arrogant and taunting tone came over the radio.

Nevan clenched his teeth together. "No. There is another animal out here, bigger than the deer."

The cat snorted. "We're all animals, Doc. I thought you were smart enough to know that."

Arrogant ass. He was about to send back his own taunt when Jared gritted out a curse out. "Fuckin' rogue!"

That phrase was all Nevan needed to push his legs as fast as they could go. "Location," he barked. No answer. "Jared!"

He skidded to a halt when a man stepped in front

of him. It took a few seconds to recognize him. "Dane, right?"

"Yeah. Jared's not responding to mind-link either." Dane shook his head. Cam had warned the male not to use it earlier, but he'd thought nothing of it.

"Jared's Cam's brother, which connects him directly to Keegan."

Nevan nodded. Now it made sense. The Enforcers had to form a blood bond with the Alpha or, in this case, both Alphas—Keegan and Luna—in order to protect the packs. The bond formed a tight inner circle that gave them the strength they needed. Apparently, mind linking was one of those strengths.

He took a step forward, only to have Dane grab his arm. "I have orders to bring you to the cabin."

Nev narrowed his eyes. "I'm going to find Jared."

Dane shook his head and growled. "You are one stubborn SOB, you know that?"

"Yep."

A howl of pain cut through the night air, sending a cold shiver up Nevan's spine. He jogged ahead, following the sound. With his senses, he searched for any sign of Jared. After a few seconds, he found a faint connection to the cat and started to run.

"Are you sure you're not a shifter?" Dane ran beside him.

"Yes, I'm sure. I was raised with them, and I'm empathic."

"Ah. That explains it."

Both of them stopped dead. Nevan's heart sped at the sight of Jared lying in the snow, barely breathing, with his throat ripped open. His blood darkened the snow around him. Nevan dropped to his knees and covered the wound.

Dane barked orders over the line. "Get Sasha, and have her at the cabin when we get there. Coming on foot. Better yet... Blaine, we need pick up."

Nevan peered at the wolf, confused. Dane shrugged. "He can teleport."

Oh, he remembered that now. Danica had mentioned it the day he'd found out the town's little secret. Ashwood Falls was full of surprises. It was exactly what he needed to get away from his grief-filled life and start over.

Blaine flashed in. "Sasha's at the house. She came in right after we left." He looked at Jared, and a tic formed in his temples. "The rogues will pay for this." He lifted Jared up off the ground, grabbed Nevan's arm, and flashed them back to the cabin.

AFTER JARED FELL silent and the radio cut off, Danica had paced her cabin. Worry ate at her. Her palms felt clammy, and her heart hurt. She didn't love Jared as a mate would, but she'd never wanted anything to happen to him. Knowledge of a rogue running around didn't ease her panic.

"I hate not knowing. Shay, can you pick up anything?"

Shay shook her head. "They blocked me."

The door flew open, making Danica whirl around to see Blaine carrying an unconscious Jared straight to the guest room. Cam and Sasha jumped up to rush after the men while Danica went to gather her medical supplies in case Sasha needed anything. It'd been a long time since her home was used as a medical facility.

When she entered the room, her chest tightened. Cam sat on the edge of the bed, holding her brother's hand in one of hers and stroking his cheek with the other, providing him with the touch a shifter needs from his family. Danica moved to the other side of the bed where Sasha worked to close up the hole in his throat.

Hovering her hand over his chest, Danica felt the

steady beat of his heart. Relief pushed away some of the tension in her body. He was going to be okay.

A FEW HOURS LATER, Danica entered the living room. Everyone, but Sasha, was still there. She'd been called back into town to tend to a couple of juveniles who'd gotten into a fight.

Cam sat up in her chair. "How is he?"

"Resting. He lost a lot of blood and needs to rest."

The jaguar nodded. "Can I see him?"

Danica nodded and Cameron stood to go see her brother.

Blaine pushed off the wall he'd been supporting to take charge of the group. "We need to get back." The other Enforcers stood, said their farewells, and left. Blaine turned to Nevan and extended his hand. "Welcome to the pack."

Confused, Nevan took his hand in a firm handshake. "I didn't win."

"No, but you reacted like a Pack member protecting his own. That shows loyalty. Plus, we need a good shrink to help the youth deal with the combining of the Packs."

Nevan smiled, making Danica's heart skip a beat. "Are you offering me a job?"

Blaine shrugged. "If you stay, you work." He nodded to Danica and dematerialized.

Danica wrung her hands in front of her. Fear of losing him hung between them. He stepped forward, cupped her face, and kissed her softly. "I guess I'm the town shrink."

All her tense feelings and insecurity melted away, and she flung her arms around him in a tight hug. "I love you, Nev."

"I love you, too. Now let's go complete this mating."

She pulled back to study him. "Are you sure? I mean it really is until death. That could be hundreds of years considering you would take my lifespan."

His smile and the wicked gleam in his gaze sent heat to her sex. "I think I can handle it."

Check out book two in Shifter of Ashwood Falls, A Tiger's Claim

A LOOK AT TIGER'S CLAIM

Shayna Andrews's paws pounded against the earth as she ran through the forest of the Smokey Mountains. Her heart thumped behind her ribs, and the cool air of early spring blew through her fur. She'd have to stop soon to catch her breath, but she didn't care. Never in her twenty-five years of life had she felt so free. And she *was* free.

For the moment.

It'd been about an hour since she'd left home to run off her anger from the heated argument she'd had with her father. When was he ever going realize that she was a grown woman, strong and capable of making decisions for herself? Sadly, she didn't think he'd ever let her have the independence she desperately craved.

So, with her emotions running high, her anger at his stubborn 'father knows best' attitude pushed her to run, even if it was just for an hour or so.

Now that she'd calmed a bit, she did find it odd that neither her brothers nor her father had come searching for her, with their worry and anger leading their way. Could they be allowing her the independence she deserved?

Maybe.

She slowed to a walk and scanned the area. This part of the woods was farther than she'd ever gone before. The forest grew thick with large trees and underbrush, while the smell of melting snow and earth wrapped around her. She inhaled deeply, relishing the natural world around her.

She was still within Ashwood territory, but several miles outside of the town she'd called home since she was two; the home in which she had always felt like a prisoner.

Sure, she was loved whole-heartedly by her adopted family and both Packs that made up Ashwood Falls, but they suffocated her.

Since the rogue attack on Jared, the town's legal counsel and close friend to her family, a couple of months before, her father—leopard Pack Alpha—had put everyone on alert. The attack itself wasn't what had scared the shit out of everyone. No, it was the fact that the mutants, half-human, half-animal rogue assassins, had gotten past the wards undetected and ripped out Jared's throat—something that was almost impossible for such a strong shifter. Jared had challenged Nevan, the leopard Healer's new mate, to a Hunt. Shay knew it was to test Nevan's strength, but she also believed Jared challenged him to see if he'd be a good mate to a leopard. Not just any leopard. Their Healer. The most loved and protected Pack member besides the princess.

Until that night, Shay never considered the true dangers of the enemy, and the lengths they would go to weaken the Ashwood Pack.

The Pack members' sense of safety had started to crumble. No one was to leave the area without an escort. That was nothing new to Shay. She always had an enforcer nearby.

But, not today.

Giddy at her escape, she shifted to her human form, her jeans and light sweater covering her body at the same time thanks to her pinky ring, which had been a gift from her father after her first shift.

The ring was made up of a small, flat, blue opal set in silver. It was enchanted to hold her clothes while she shifted. All she had to do was think a small invocation at the same time she called her tiger and her clothes dissolved inside the stone. Somehow, the magick in the ring was in tune to her aura because the moment she changed back to human form her clothes reappeared.

She inhaled, drawing in the crisp mountain air. It was mid-March, and even though the full effects of spring were another month away, the forest already held the signs of new life. Snow was starting to melt in some places, and the trees were starting to bud. Even the air held notes of new life—the earth, trees, and the hint of floral no longer incased in ice.

A snap of a twig in the distance put her tiger on alert. Her heart thumped wildly in her chest. She sniffed the air and picked up on a musk and rosemary scent that was unfamiliar to her. Fear burned through her veins, and she started to head back to town, wishing for once that her brothers were lurking nearby.

Okay, Shay, you're being a baby.

Closing her eyes, she calmed herself and recalled all the brutal training Blaine and Alec had put her through over the years. The hand-to-hand training was a precaution in case Ashwood Falls was attacked. Father had scowled at the bruises and cuts on her when they returned home, but her brothers brushed it off. In their defense, they claimed she needed to be trained like a soldier.

Blaine and Alec not only taught her how to fight, they taught her to draw strength from the elements around her because they believed she possessed witch's blood.

It was true she could perform simple spells and make potions from herbs, but that was the extent of her so-called magickal abilities. However, she'd learned to connect with the earth and air around her. That connection allowed her to sense danger, like now.

Whoever, or whatever, was out there was closing in fast. She felt the eerie caress of danger against her aura. It made her tiger growl. This was so not good.

Please be an animal of some kind and not the rogue mutant kind.

She jogged ahead, not taking any chance in the event rogues had trespassed on Ashwood territory again. They'd ripped a whole through Jared's throat, and he was a very strong alpha male. She didn't want to hang out to see what they would do to her, a lone female, who despite all she wished, wasn't as strong as she wanted to be.

Footfalls edged closer, putting her tiger on full alert. She ran faster. Several yards ahead, a man stepped into her path. She skidded to a halt and realized he wasn't a man, but a mutant—half-wolf, half-man—and abomination. The rancid smell of spoiled meat lingered behind the vague scent of rosemary and another smell she wasn't familiar reached out to her thick and oily-like. His long, sharp claws extended from his fingertips, and his fangs elongated until they reached his chin. His eyes were the deepest brown she'd ever seen, almost black, matching his dark fur.

Wolf-man took a step forward, and Shay moved with him, backing up until she hit a solid wall of muscle. Hot fear burned in her belly and spread to her chest as a pair of clawed hands wrapped around her biceps. She sensed others lurking nearby, but she didn't want to take her gaze from the mutant in front of her. A male in human form stepped into view and stood shoulder-to-shoulder with the mutant in front of her.

Her heart raced as she struggled to push down the bile that rose in her throat. By their dilated pupils, she guessed they were on some kind of drug.

So not good.

She jerked, trying to break the male's grip. He laughed and tightened his hold, making his claws sink into her skin. She bit back the sharp pain, refusing to show them any weakness. When the male's lips touched her cheek, she winced and tried not to be sick.

"Look what we have here, boys."

The rancid smell of his breath intensified her nausea. She jerked side to side again, trying to break his hold, his claws tearing into her skin that much deeper. He didn't budge. The burning fear turned to ice in her veins as she stared at two males stalking toward her with a lusty hunger in their eyes.

Death wouldn't come quick enough if she couldn't get away.

Wolf-man tilted his head to the side and snarled to make his elongated fangs appear longer under the moonlight. "She sure is a pretty kitty. And I bet she'd be fun to play with before we kill her."

Fucking bastards.

She had to think, outwit them somehow.

When wolf-man stopped inches from her face, her heart rate stuttered then raced as though it were trying to run away. He smiled, showing blood-stained teeth. Her dinner from an hour before threatened to reappear, and her skin moistened from sweat. She tried to kick him, but he caught her leg in his clawed hand.

Stupid, stupid, Shay.

The male holding her yanked her out of the other wolf's grasp, pulling her hip out of place with an audible snap. She screamed as the pain shot through her, a vile agony that warred with her emotions. Tears stung her eyes. She tried to breathe through the pain, her leg practically useless.

There would be no running. Not anymore.

"You two go back to the den," the male behind her demanded. "I'll take care of our guest."

They didn't move and the human-like rogue shook his head. "You're not having her to yourself."

She started to shake. Adrenaline rushed through her blood, fueling the tiger's need to fight, to hurt, to kill. Her fangs pushed through her gums, and her fingernails lengthened to claws. She reached around her and gripped the wolf's balls, sinking her sharp nails into his flesh.

With a howl, the male pushed her away, forcing her to the ground. She managed to scramble to stand on her good leg and hobbled away from them while dragging her useless limb behind her.

But, it was no use.

She was too far from home. She couldn't mind link with her family or the enforcers at this distance. No one would know anything until it was too late.

The male in human form suddenly tackled her to the ground. He flipped her to her back to straddle over her, putting pressure on her dislocated hip. The scream ripped from her throat and she slashed her claws down his chest. The bastard laughed and bared his teeth. She slapped his face with her lengthened nails, leaving four deep gashes across his cheek.

When he turned back to her, she gasped at the way his eyes glowed in anger. A wolf howled in the distance, freezing her blood. More were coming. She locked gazes with the wolf above her and knew he would finish her. He raised his clawed hand and swiped it across her face, then back-handed her on the other side. The scratches burned as warm blood ran down her cheek. He hit her again, harder, and all sounds and sights around her faded as she drifted into the darkness.

BLAINE ANDREWS SCOWLED at the section of barbwire blocking off a part of Ashwood's property. It was the same area of the woods the Pack Healer, Danica, had been trapped in several months before. He clenched his teeth together and ground his molars.

Beside him, Cameron fidgeted with the snap on her thigh holster, a nervous gesture she did when she itched to shoot something or someone. Usually he would let it go, let her fume, but today they weren't going into battle. They were investigating suspicious activity called in by a couple of the adolescents.

He clamped his hand over Cam's, stilling her endless snap-unsnap of the holster. "Stop or I'll give you something to fondle."

She leaned into him, pressing her lips to his ear. "You promise?" she purred. He was nanoseconds away from dragging her into the forest to give her exactly what she taunted him with. Fast and hard, exactly what they both needed right now.

The clearing of a throat made him raise an eyebrow at the newest resident of Ashwood Falls, a human named Nevan Mathews, Danica's mate and the head shrink in town. "You have problems, empathy?"

Nevan's mouth twitched. "Nope. Just want to get back to my own mate."

Blaine laughed then frowned as uneasiness settled in his blood. Cam stiffened beside him and he asked, "You feel that?"

Cam nodded. "Something's not right."

He connected telepathically with his brother, who was in town setting up surveillance cameras with Dane—one of the wolf enforcers. *"Have you heard from Shay? Is she back from her run?"*

"No, I haven't seen her."

Fuck. He knew he should have placed someone on her trail and never let her go out alone. But, damn it, she was twenty-five years old, an adult and fully capable of taking care of herself.

"Blaine, she'll show when she cools down."

Alec was right. Shayna had to learn to be on her own, even though their father didn't see it that way. *"I know. How are the security cameras coming?"*

Alec laughed. *"Great. We just caught the Russell twins sneaking around Nevan and Dani's new place."*

"Those two are always in trouble. Go see what they're up to."

"We're on it."

Blaine dropped the link with Alec and peered at Nevan. "The twins are sneaking around your new home." As a mating gift, Keegan was having a house built in town for the happy couple.

Nevan shook his head. "Last week they put mud in the drain pipes."

"When do you two move in?" Cameron asked.

Blaine slid his gaze toward her at the hint of joy in her statement. Despite her dominance and ability to kick ass along with the rest of the enforcers, she loved her family and friends. And she also loved to drive him to the brink of insanity and need. What frustrated him the most was the fact that she wouldn't complete the mating. They were mates. There was no denying it, yet she was still waiting for something. Blaine didn't push because he, too, felt as though something was off, or missing, in their lives.

Nevan checked his watch. Blaine wasn't sure if it was out of habit or he was meeting Dani somewhere. "In about two days. Construction is finished. Dani wants to paint the inside herself."

Blaine cast a glance around the forest then back at the barbwire fence. "We'll have to find a witch or two to strengthen the wards." He fisted his hands at his sides then turned toward his truck.

He heard Nevan following him. Blaine allowed a smile to spread across his face. The human didn't like being teleported, so Blaine had offered to drive. Stopping at the driver's side door, he peered over at Cameron. "Call Dane to help with that."

She waved her hand at him in a dismissing manner and ripped the fence out of the ground then proceeded to roll it up. Blaine shook his head. *Damn stubborn jaguar.*

Before climbing into his truck, he tensed. A female scream cut into his thoughts, and a cold sensation went up his spine the same time as a sharp pain stabbed his temple. Staggering back several feet, he swung around to find himself nose-to-nose with Cameron.

Dead fear shown in her dark gaze. "Shay. Something's happened…"

His heart pounded fiercely behind his ribcage as he reached for Cam and tried to think.

"Blaine, man? What is it?" It didn't surprise Blaine that Nevan could sense something was wrong. He was an empath after all.

Blaine tossed his keys to him. "Go tell Keegan that Cam and I are searching for Shay and to send backup."

Cameron was the first to shift. Her clothes dissolved as a soft flash of white light completed the transition from woman to black jaguar. Blaine shifted into his leopard and ran beside her through the forest at supernatural speeds, following their instincts and the faint connection to his adopted sister.

He prayed like hell he found her alive.

Shifter of Ashwood Falls

After losing over half of their dens to a group rogue shifters, the wolves and leopards merged as one Pack, but living together is much more of a challenge then they expected.

Series Reading Order
Winter Eve
A Tiger's Claim
A Mating Dance
Surrendering to the Alpha
A Rebel's Heart
Divided Loyalties
Touch of Desire
A Leopard's Path
Jaguar's Judgment
Bundles of Pink (A short story)
Alpha Challenge
Mating Chaos
A Tiger for Two
Claimed by the Alpha

Bundle and save

Get 30% off all 14 books: https://davisraynesbooks.
com/products/ashood-falls-bundle

ABOUT THE AUTHOR

USA Today bestselling author Lia Davis spends most of her time writing racy romance and witty women's fiction, the majority of which takes place in fantasy worlds full of magic and mayhem. She prides herself on her ability to craft strong and sassy heroines, emotionally intelligent alpha heroes, and rich, expansive universes that readers want to visit again and again.

She is the mastermind behind the bestselling Ashwood Falls Series and the co-author of the beloved Witching After Forty Series.

She currently resides in Florida where she's working on her very own happily-ever-after with her supportive husband and spends her free time doting on a pack of feisty felines and her loving family.

Find all of Lia's online hang outs here: https://solo.to/authorliadavis

Check out the official Davis Raynes Merch Esty Store: https://www.etsy.com/shop/davisraynesmerch

ALSO BY LIA DAVIS

Paranormal Women's Fiction / Cozy Mysteries

Witching After Forty (Co-written with L.A. Boruff)

Fanged After Forty (Co-written with L.A. Boruff)

Hunting After Forty (Co-written with L.A. Boruff)

Shifting Through Midlife (Co-written with L.A. Boruff and Lacey Carter)

Sisterhood of the Stones (Co-written with L.A. Boruff and Lacey Carter)

Cornellis Island (Co-written with L.A. Boruff and Lacey Carter)

Bellarose Cat Cafe (Co-written with L.A. Boruff and Lacey Carter)

Packless in Seattle

Howling Creek Mysteries

Urban Fantasy

Randi Sanderson Series

Blood Omen (part of the Accidental Zodiacs World)

Paranormal Romance Series

Shifters of Ashwood Falls

Bears of Blackrock

Dark Scales Division (Co-written with Kerry Adrienne)

Shifting Magick Trilogy

The Divinities

Witches of Rose Lake

Coven's End (Co-written with L.A. Boruff)

Academy's Rise (Co-written with L.A. Boruff)

Wolves of Kelmount Ranch

<u>*Singles Titles*</u>

First Contact (MM co-written with Kerry Adrienne)

Ghost in the Bottle (co-written with Kerry Adrienne)

Dragon's Web

Royal Enchantment

Marked by Darkness

His Big Bad Wolf (MM)

Their Royal Ash

Tempting the Wolf

Rogue Alliance (Part of the Wolves of Chaos Valley Shared World)

Rune of Passing (Part of the Immortal Keepers Shared World)